MW01610147

Operation Betty

William Conder AMS³

William Conder (signature)

Operation Betty

ISBN: 979-8-89075-000-6

Operation Betty

Contents

Operation Betty

"As long as there are sovereign nations possessing great power, war is inevitable."

-Albert Einstein

Dedication

Dedicated to all the veterans, past, present, and future. May fair winds and following seas bring you home safe.

About the Author

William Conder is a Gulf War veteran who served four years in the Navy at HSL-42 NAS Mayport, Florida, working on SH-60B helicopters.

His time in the Navy took him halfway around the world aboard the USS Normandy and USS McInerney, allowing him to see and do many things.

He currently works for the U.S. Army Corps of Engineers as an operator and former diver, where he now lives in Illinois with his wife, Dawn. They have one daughter named Courtney.

PROLOGUE

Kentucky 1924

"Mom, I'm going down to Old Man Ray's house to see if he needs any help." An energetic, thirteen-year-old Jonathan said as he was putting on his shoes as fast as his little fingers would allow him to get them tied and out the door before his mother could tell him no. He was at that stage in life where everything he learns now will sculpt and mold him into the man he is to become.

"Now, Jonathan Stephen McKendree, what have I told you about calling him Old Man Ray? You address him as Mister Ray and show him some respect, or you won't go anywhere but to your room. Do you understand me, young man? Make sure you are home before dark. The last time you were down there so late, I thought I would have to come and get you. You were down there way too long, and I don't want you bugging Mister Ray and making him upset."

"But Mom, I told him I would be down there today to help him with the firewood, and he would show me how to work on his old crop duster. I'm sure he needs me to help with some other things too."

"Mmmhmm. I know better than that. I'm sure you are going down there hoping he will take you for a ride in that old terrible excuse for an airplane. I've told you that I don't like you bugging him and asking him to take you flying in that dinosaur of a plane. It's unsafe, and I don't want you to get hurt."

"But Moooom!" Jonathan let out in a pleading voice. "We never fly very high, and it's only for a few minutes. I always help him with extra chores to make up for the time he takes me flying. One of these days, I'd like to work on airplanes or maybe even be a pilot. Wouldn't that be great?"

"Now, Jonathan McKendree, you need to get your head out of the clouds. Go ahead and take this food down there to him and help him with whatever he needs you to do with no fussing, and then you get right back home. Do you understand me, young man? Don't be bugging him with any of your foolishness. You still have plenty of chores to finish here before the end of the day."

Beth McKendree stood at their two-bedroom shack's old worn-out screen door, watching her son heading up the dirt road towards Old Man Rays. She wondered if raising Jonathan alone was such a good idea now. His father dying when he was just five years old made it hard when Jonathan asked about him. She had noticed that he has been asking about his father less frequently since he spends more time with Old Man Ray. Still, she was not sure if that was such a good thing. On the other hand, she realized that Jonathan did need a father figure in his life.

February 4th,1945

It was dark that night. The mist carried gloom, and the smell of petrichor lingered in the air. The entire city was asleep; the lights were dim, and nothing could be heard in the distance. A streetlight flickered now and then, and the wind in the man's hair, hesitantly walking the puddles on the streets, grew stronger as he approached an open area.

He looked around, and no one could be seen, not even a silhouette of a man. He pulled out a chained watch from his pocket and looked at the time; he was early. He still had a few minutes on his hands. Suddenly, he heard footsteps as a calm before the storm. They quickly grew louder as they approached from behind him. The man fixed the round hat as he turned.

The man was standing right in front of him with an earnest look. He wore a long coat just like his and carried a briefcase. The man studied him for a while and put the briefcase down. He then nodded and turned, walking into a dark alley from where he came from. In silence, each one there to complete a given task and then go their separate ways.

12

The man with the hat picked up the briefcase behind him and walked in the opposite direction. While walking, he pulled out the watch again and disappeared into a dark alley where his car was parked.

With every second that passed, the fog kept getting thicker and thicker, and finally, after the sky poured a drizzle, two headlights illuminated the spot where the briefcase was dropped; it was the man with the hat. He put his car in gear and drove on the highway to the airbase.

When the man arrived at the airbase, he parked his car and got out with a suitcase in one hand and the briefcase in the other. Anxiously, he waited before he was finally allowed to board the plane. His briefcase documents were top secret, and his mission was dangerous. Destination? Dubendorf airfield.

Fortunately, he was recommended just the right person to escort him there – First Lieutenant McKendree.

Chapter 1
The Call

Fast forward to the year 1985. As the sun set and the shadows of the night became more abstruse, fading lights of the evening sky submerged into the cold, bleak winter night. The atmosphere is soaked in the dead of winter. The flickering lampposts lined the road and lit the pathway for the passers-by. The sky gently dropped snowflakes upon the surface. The mystique of nature ensured that not a single snowflake resembled another. Some snowflakes managed to touch the ground while the branches of the leafless trees captured others. The wind sang the ballads of life as it blew through the deserted streets of the night, with the beats of the saddest notes, carrying the stories of life and death, sorrow and pain, agony and joy. There is something mysterious about winter; it is a symphony of unexplained sorrow.

Inside, the sounds of a crackling fire burning in the hearth soothed the atmosphere while the kettle rested on the stove boiling the post-dinner tea.

A pair of intrigued eyes occupied the windowpane; an older man gazed through the window and observed the wandering people in pursuit of searching the night. He could hear the echoes produced by the wheels of cars. A slight screech was produced from the cars speeding the empty roads; white frosted smoke projected from their tailpipes. The older man continued to gaze through the window pane while the night was young; he was deeply invested in the view, awaiting the arrival of his son Karl, whom he had phoned just yesterday.

"Lisa, are you there?" the old man called out.

With the phone against her ear, Lisa answered, "Yes, sir. I am right here. Is there anything I can help you with? Perhaps a glass of water?"

The old man coughed again and murmured, "Yes, please." As he laid back down on the bed.

Lisa then rushed to the kitchen to fetch a glass of water for the dying man. "Here you go, sir," she said. Lisa held the glass near his mouth while the man lifted his head and drank from it. "Careful," Lisa mumbled.

"Aaaaaah!" The older man felt relieved. "Lisa?"

"Yes, sir?" she answered.

"Is he coming?" he asked.

Confused, Lisa nodded. "Yes, he must be on his way here now," she lied.

"Lisa, you know I can tell when a person is lying. Please tell me the truth. It is not right to lie to a dying old man," Jonathan said.

Lisa, who didn't know what to say, gathered herself and looked the man in the eye. "I assure you, sir. Karl is coming. I just haven't gotten in touch with him since yesterday."

The man softly chuckled, laid back, and closed his eyes. "He is coming," he mumbled.

Lisa returned to the living room and waited desperately with the phone in her hand. She was walking back and forth, waiting for Karl to call.

Suddenly, the phone in her hands rang. Lisa answered it on the first ring. "Hello?" she answered.

"Lisa? This is Karl. Is everything okay?"

Lisa took a deep breath of relief and said, "Yes, everything is alright. But your dad, he keeps asking for you... he wants to know if you're coming. I am afraid he doesn't have long."

"Well, don't worry. My wife and I will be on our way. We can be there tonight. Until then, just keep an eye on him, Lisa."

As Karl hung up the phone, he turned to his wife, Julia, and said, "I am afraid, dear, we will have to catch the next available flight out. Dad doesn't have much time."

Karl and Julia quickly packed their bags and left the house.

Julia, in the passenger seat, nodded. "Alright, the nearest airport is about five miles from here, and according to the GPS, we can make it there in 15 minutes, max."

"Perfect, just let me know where to go from here."

"Take a left, and then drive straight to Tatum Blvd," she instructed.

Karl put the car in gear and carefully drove through the traffic, taking a left onto Tatum Blvd. As he drove, Julia could sense the tension at the back of his mind. She held his hand and reassured him, "Karl, everything is going to be okay; you know that, right?"

Karl looked at his wife, nodded, and pinned his sight back to the road. "Thanks, honey," he said and drove straight to the airport, thinking about what his dad wanted to tell him now, after all these years, as Lisa told him on the phone.

Chapter 2

The Army Air Corps

"Come on in, Karl. You are just in time," greeted Lisa Stevens, Jonathan's nurse, as she opened the door to let Karl in. "I just got your father up for lunch," she added.

"How is he doing today, Lisa? Is he feeling any better? Karl asked with a concerned look on his face.

"Oh, he is doing a lot better now that we have his medications adjusted and gotten him on a routine. I just caught him in there daydreaming again. I would say his condition has improved a lot. He has been asking for you and wondering when you would get here."

"I wonder what is so important this time?"

"You know your dad; there is no telling. I think he is just trying to get his affairs in order. I reckon he's afraid he doesn't have much time left. With cancer, you just don't know how much time you have. Did your family get to come with you today?"

"Well…kind of. My wife Julia did, but the boys are back at college. They may be here this weekend. Julia is getting the rest of her things from the car, and she will be right in."

From the living room, Jonathan yelled out, "Karl, is that you? Did the boys come with you?"

"Yes, it's me, Dad, and no, the boys didn't come this time, unfortunately. They are busy with college. I will be in there shortly. I am just waiting for Julia to come in."

"Well, I am done for the day. If he needs anything urgent, call me, and I will come. My number is on the fridge. I will be back in the morning to check on your dad. Goodbye and take care," Lisa stated and left.

When Julia finally entered the house, they both made their way into the living room to see what was so urgent with Jonathan.

As they entered the room, they saw that Jonathan was sitting upright in the hospital bed they had set up for him in the living room. He seemed to have been anxiously waiting for Karl and the family to come in with a concerned look on his face.

"Okay, Dad, we are here. So, what is so urgent?"

"I need to tell you something very important that your mother had always wanted to but never got the chance before she died. She made me promise that I would tell you someday before I died. I think, son, it's about time you knew the truth. Since I'm not sure how much time I have left."

"The truth about what? What's the big secret?"

There was a brief pause before Jonathan responded to Karl's question.

"It's a long story and one we should have told you when you were younger. I never knew how you would feel about me if I told you the truth."

"Dad, is this another one of your war stories? Or is this about how you weren't a cook during the war and were on a secret mission flying a plane? We have heard all of this before."

Jonathan was visibly unamused at Karl's jesting.

"Karl, will you be quiet for a few minutes and let me tell you what I need to say before this lung cancer kills me? This is important. And no, this isn't just another one of my war stories."

"Okay, okay. What is it you need to tell me? I'm all ears."

"Karl, do you remember what I told you about how your mother and I met?"

"Yes. You always told me you met mom after you got out of the service, and then you got married. You said she worked down at the local diner you often went to and that it was love at first sight."

"That's what we always told you, but that wasn't the truth. Yes, I fell in love with her the first time I laid eyes on her, but I wasn't sure she felt the same about me at the time. Our meeting was much more complicated than that, and it wasn't in a diner. Believe me. I'm not sure many people have met the way we did," Jonathan said with a slight chuckle.

Karl said, with a confused look on his face. "Dad, what are you talking about? How did you and mom meet, then?"

"Sit down and have a seat while I tell you the real story of how I met your mother. It all started in the winter of 1941 after Japan bombed Pearl Harbor and the United States entered World War II. Everyone took the attack on American soil personally and wanted to help with the war effort. And just like everyone else, I wanted to join the military to help too. I figured that, with the knowledge of working on car engines and the few times I had worked on Old Man Ray's crop duster, I could get a job in the military working on airplanes. I figured they would need mechanics to keep the planes flying. So, it was July 1942, and I went to the local recruiting office to enlist in the United States Army Air Corps. Sure enough, they had openings for aircraft mechanics if you scored high enough. Surprisingly, I scored well above the minimum score needed for the job. I was elated. I signed my enlistment papers, and I was on my way. Little did I know they had made a mistake on my enlistment papers and enlisted me as a cook instead of an aircraft mechanic!"

"Now, wait a minute, Dad. You always told us that you were a cook in the military. So, when did you ever work on crop dusters, who was this 'Old Man Ray,' and why haven't I heard of him before?"

"Okay, okay. Hang on. I told you it was a long story. I will explain it as best I can. I'm not sure what his last name was. I just always knew him as Old Man Ray. Your grandmother Beth always used to get so mad at me for calling him that. It's funny now that I think about it. I haven't thought of him in so many years. Now with the memories returning, I would say I miss him. I wish you could have met him, son. He was like a father to me back then. He lived just down the road from our house, and your grandma used to let me go down to his house to work on his farm in trade for some food and him fixing things for us. He got to where he would teach me how to work on engines and occasionally take me up in his crop duster.

I always used to love to go up flying with him in that old crop duster of his. There's no experience on earth like flying those old planes, son. When you take to the skies, you feel the wind blowing in your hair, and the smell of clean, crisp air mixed with burning oil is separate altogether. I learned a lot from Ray, and I think we enjoyed one another's company. He didn't have any kids or a wife, and I didn't have a father, so it kind of worked out for the both of us. Your grandfather died when I was about five years old. So, at the age of thirteen, the age at about which a boy needs his father, Old Man Ray, just happened to be the one I clung to at that time. He was the one that taught me all the things that boys usually learn from their fathers. Where do you think I learned some of the things that I taught you when you were that age?"

Jonathan could see that he now had his son's full attention and was assured he wouldn't make any wisecrack remarks to ruin his narration.

Chapter 3
The Mix-Up

"Now, let me get back to what happened. I have never told you this part of the story, and now I think it's time I finally told you everything," Jonathan continued.

"Okay, Dad, let's hear it. You have me all curious now. This should be a good one, like the rest of your stories," Karl stated as he and his wife took a seat on the couch across from Jonathan's bed.

"As I said, I had just gotten my enlistment papers, and it wasn't until I was on my way to Montgomery, Alabama, for my school to be an aircraft mechanic that they told me that my papers said that I had enlisted as a cook. I was flabbergasted. I told them there must be some mistake because I enlisted as an aircraft mechanic. I kept insisting on being let inside the school. Seeing my persistence, they looked at my papers and noticed that the MOS (Military Occupational Specialty) for an aircraft mechanic was one number different from a cook. The MOS for an aircraft mechanic was 6, and the MOS for a cook was 60. It was realized that the secretary typing my papers had accidentally added a zero! Can you believe that? Just my luck. I always thought I had bad luck, but this was the worst. Sadly, at that point, there wasn't much that could be done about it. I was stuck as a cook. They told me it would be almost impossible to fix and that I'd be better off just doing my time and not fighting it. So, instead of further fighting their mix-up to no avail, I decided to take my lumps and do my time. That way, I reasoned, maybe I could still do some good while I was in by helping feed everyone. Or at least, so I thought."

"Now, Dad, is this true? It was all a mix-up, and you should have been an aircraft mechanic instead?" Karl questioned with loads of doubt in his voice. "Mom had always agreed that you were a cook in the army. Why lie? It doesn't matter what job anyone had during that time. Everyone was needed to help make a difference, even cooks. Dad, I am proud of you for signing up and joining during the war," he added.

"I am getting to that if you will let me. So, yes, I started out as a cook, and that's what we always told you, but that's not where I was by the time I was finished with my enlistment. That is the story your mother and I had agreed to tell you at the time. It was just an easier way to explain how we met without going into great detail and you asking questions. But now that you are all grown up, and I am close to death, I think it is time I told you the complete story of what happened. Better now than never."

"Please, Dad. Tell me everything this time, and don't leave anything out."

"I will. So, where was I? Ah, yes, so now I was officially on my way to school to be a cook. Obviously, I wasn't as excited about this school as I was about the aircraft mechanic school. Truth be told, I knew absolutely nothing at all about cooking. I had always spent my time under a hood working on engines, not in the kitchen playing Betty Crocker. I learned just enough to get by and move on. I was just excited to be in the military trying to do my part and make a difference in the Allied war effort."

As Jonathan reflects on that time in his life, one can truly see how much he missed the feeling of being needed and the camaraderie with all of his fellow soldiers. It was not unlike how most military veterans feel as they reminisce about the most important years of their lives. The part of their life when they felt needed and wanted, even if it's for a few short years—the most consequential time in a serviceman's life.

"I don't regret my few short months of being a cook because it not only allowed me to meet some amazing people that remained my friends throughout my time in the military and even after I was discharged. I hadn't been out of my cooking school very long, and being the new guy, I was sent on all kinds of silly errands. This one time, I was sent to the other side of the base to pick up some boxes of food and cooking supplies that were accidentally delivered to the wrong building. How in the world do you send food and cooking supplies to a flight training school building? It seems like the military was always messing things up. Anyway, while I was there inquiring about the boxes of food and supplies, it seemed my luck had finally changed because I was approached by an officer asking me if I knew anything about airplanes. After telling him my short version of what happened with my disastrous job assignment of going from aircraft mechanic to cook, I proceeded to ask him why. He told me they were short on bodies for the next flight class and needed one more body to continue. He asked me if I would be interested in signing up for the class since I had some experience with aircraft. Boy, was I excited at that offer!"

At that, Jonathan paused and became lost in his thoughts.

"Dad?"

"Huh?

"You were telling us about the offer."

"Hmm…. oh right, I couldn't tell him yes fast enough. Talk about being in the right place at the right time. I hurried back to the mess hall with the boxes of food and cooking supplies to tell the other guys what had happened and that I would be transferred to the flight school at the beginning of the next week. I was so excited and couldn't believe how my luck had changed. And quite frankly, neither could they. Everyone in the mess hall thought I was pulling their leg and playing a joke on them. Later that day, that same officer came by with my transfer papers, enrolling me in the next flight class. That was the last of my mess hall days. I was beyond excited, but this isn't to say I found my time as a cook all that bad. I still ran into some of the guys I worked with at the mess hall until I graduated and got transferred to another base."

Again, Jonathan paused and got lost in his thoughts.

Chapter 4
Flight School

"Dad, please continue."

"Yes…sorry about that, son. Your dad has gotten old, and it is hard not to get distracted while reminiscing about one of the greatest times of my life. Right…hmm…coming back to the story. Getting accepted into the flight school was like a lifelong dream come true. I remember telling your grandmother I wanted to be a pilot or work on airplanes. My time with Old Man Ray sparked that part in me as a child and stayed with me for the rest of my life. And now I was finally getting the chance to live my dream. It's all I ever wanted as I spent those days with him, flying up in the sky and feeling the wind in my face pretending to be chasing Germans and shooting them down. Now here I was, finally getting my chance."

Now Jonathan could see a spark in Karl's eyes – the same spark he had as a kid whenever Jonathan shared his stories during bedtime.

"Though just because I was passionate and had some prior flight experience didn't mean the whole school journey went like a breeze. The flight school was tough, but the guys in the class helped me a lot and ensured I learned everything I needed to get through the class. We were all close and stuck together like a family. One Friday night after class, a bunch of the guys asked me if I wanted to go out and have a few drinks at the bar and look for Betties. I wasn't well-acquainted with military slang, so I asked them what a Betty was. They said it was their term for a woman. They also said you might find your wife if you found the right Betty. They always went out every weekend after class looking for their perfect Betty.

I wasn't all that interested in love and romance at the time. My mind was preoccupied with the war effort and acing flight school. I decided I'd tag along for fun to have something to do, but I don't remember if any of them ever found what they were looking for, honestly. I know I never did. One of the things that I do remember was our class motto. It was 'Fly 'em High, Do or Die.' I will never forget it as long as I live.

Hmm...now, coming back to the story. Even though our class was coming in near the war's end, we were still hardcore and would have given our lives for any of our newfound brothers in that class. The one guy I remember the most and whom I was closest to was Harry Thompson. He was smart, the top of his class, and well-mannered but, most notably, extremely humble. He was the one that helped me the most during flight school. I probably wouldn't have made it if it wasn't for him. I'm not sure why he took such an interest in me, but I'm glad he did and the fact that I had a chance to get to know him. For you see, I found out later after the war that he had been shot down during a mission, and they never recovered his body. I wish we could have met up after the war, just to see each other again and talk about old times. Out of everyone I met in the military while I was in, I sure do miss him the most. He was like the brother that I never had.

Jonathan again got lost in his thoughts. This time, there was visible sadness in his countenance. But, after a brief pause, he took a sip of his water and then resumed his story.

"I remember that he had a girl named Susan Mason, that he was sweet on a few towns over. He dearly missed her during his stay at flight school, but the problem was he couldn't just go and meet her. You see, land transport was still slow, and planes hadn't been commercialized yet...well, at least that's how I remember it. And it was too far for us to drive and be back by the end of the weekend. But no biggie; I, Harry, and a few other guys hatched a plan. We would borrow a B-25 Mitchell that we had sitting around the airfield that they didn't use much and fly it during the weekend. Was it risky? Yes. Was it stupid? Absolutely. If we got caught...that might have been the end of our journey at flight school. But you see, and to reiterate, we saw ourselves as more than friends – we all shared a strong brotherly bond.

And, let me tell you...it wasn't even a one-time affair. We took that B-25 many times during our stay at flight school to Susan's place. We used to land it in an old cornfield just outside the edge of town so that Harry could see his girl for the weekend. Just one of the perks of being a pilot at the time. In fact, looking back, we used to do a lot of things during that time that would probably get you court-martialed today. I always wondered what happened to Susan. I had almost forgotten about her until now. It has been so long since I have thought about her and Harry. I am sure they would have gotten married if he had made it through the war. But I guess that's the thing about the war, son. It brought the most unlikely people together and kept the most likely people apart. Crazy how that always works in life. The B-25 was always my favorite flying plane while I was in the Army Air Corps. I just always loved how it looked and how it handled." Jonathan said.

"Wow, Dad...that's absolutely amazing. I would never have thought you did all that crazy stuff in your youth," expressed Karl.

"Typical Karl...always underestimating his old man!"

"No, Dad...I didn't mean it like th-"

"Easy, son. I am just joking with you. So, after we graduated and got our wings, they split us up and sent us to different bases. I hoped they would send Harry and me to the same base, but they didn't. I never saw Harry or the rest of them again."

Karl could see that his dad had that deep nostalgic look in his eyes as if he had just lost his best friend again for the second time.

Jonathan could read the expression on Karl's face and gave off a remark: "We are always wondering where the time has gone. Like they always say, blink, and the time is gone before you know it. Time always moves fastest in our lives when we least want it to and slowest when we need it to. It's like we always wish our lives away and then want that time back after it is gone. Knowing there is no way of getting back lost time, make the most of every minute and make them count."

"Well said," Karl approved.

"Coming back, after we all said our goodbyes and went our separate ways, I was bounced around from base to base. Towards the war's end, they mostly had me deliver planes to different destinations and drop them off until after 1945. Then they transferred me to the 14th Fighter

Squadron of the 15th Air Corps stationed in Tunisia, but we ended up flying missions out of Italy. You may have heard of its first general, General Jimmy Doolittle. Forget that no-nonsense, rigid stereotype you tend to see in Hollywood of military brass. Jimmy was nothing like that. He was a great guy and would do anything for you. I got to meet him a few times.

I remember Jimmy Doolittle telling us about one mission where they flew over the Leaning Tower of Pisa, and there was a gunner set up in the tower. One of the pilots broke away from the formation and headed towards the tower, and Jimmy asked. 'Hey, what are you doing?'

He said I'm going to shoot that gunner set up in that tower. I'm tired of getting shot at. To this, Jimmy said, "No, you can't do that. That is the Leaning Tower of Pisa, you idiot!" So, on their way back, that same gunner was still set up in the tower, and he ended up shooting the one pilot in the wing. The pilot lost some control of his plane, and all he could do was fly in circles. So, he ended up having to fly back to base doing circles for an hour.

When they got back to base, obviously, he was mad, and he told Jimmy while pointing at his damaged plane, 'See, you should have let me shoot him the first time when we went through.'

Jimmy just laughed, that well-known laugh of his. 'Yeah, and the world would have lost a national landmark!' he said.

They all just laughed about how the Leaning Tower of Pisa was almost destroyed because of some new trigger-happy pilot. It's funny how just one little thing of being in the right place at the right time or the wrong place at the wrong time can change someone's life so much…or, for that matter, of many.

"Well, you can thank old Jimmy for that! I just wish I could have gone on the raid with him, but I didn't have enough flight hours at the time," explained Jonathan.

Chapter 5
Dresden Firebombing

"When the P-39 was first deployed, few of our guys were amicable towards flying this bird. You see, it had a rather unusual design for a Western aircraft. Its engine was installed in the center fuselage, behind the pilot, and because it lacked a turbocharger, it was dangerous to fly at high altitudes. Anyway, I was one of the unlucky few that were selected to fly the plane…to Dresden, deep in the heart of the enemy territory."

Karl was loaded with questions. "So, what happened? Did you get shot at?"

"Patience, son…let me continue with what happened on this mission in Dresden," Jonathan said, then paused to ensure there would be no more interruptions.

"Hmm…so where was I? Ah yes, to tell you the truth, crashing and getting captured by the Germans was, in fact, the optimistic scenario I had in my mind when I was forced to fly that plane on the mission. Yet, as I took that bird on a test flight, all my apprehensions withered away. Sure, it did not have the speed and agility of a conventional fighter plane, but that was because it wasn't one. It was built for low-altitude engagement and packed more than enough power to give any other fighter plane a run for its money. To better explain it to you youngsters, think of it as the same difference between a Kawasaki motorcycle and a Harley cruiser. My mission was to help escort bombers during the planned firebombing of Dresden. As I was given my briefings, the merit of the P-39's sturdy design became apparent in my mind. I had approached the plane with nothing but reluctance, but I was going to fly it on the mission with nothing but confidence."

"So, Dad…"

"What, son?"

"How…do you feel about the firebombing?" Karl asked with a bit of difficulty.

"Karl…I am glad you asked that…and I believe that as the end of my life draws ever closer, it is high time I make peace with my demons. Yes, killing enemy combatants is one thing, but partaking in the firebombing of civilians, many of whom were innocent women and children...that is a burden I have carried with me all these years."

Jonathan then went into deep thought, reflecting on the past.

"To tell you the truth, nothing about the war was glamorous....sure we were the 'good guys,' and I am glad we fought in the war to defeat the disgusting Nazis, but...there were some things along the way we had to do and maybe shouldn't have....war isn't glamorous, and I wish that part of it would just disappear from my memory...."

Jonathan took a brief pause to look out the window and then turned his attention back to his son and Julia.

"Well...the past is the past...let us continue with the story. It was the winter of 1945, and the Germans quickly lost ground to the Allies. To speed up our road to victory, we were to strike deep inside the German 'redoubt' of Saxony, which had still remained largely unscathed and where most of the country's military industries operated from. To be honest, son, it was total overkill. Some 2000 allied fighter planes and bombers were deployed for the mission, opposed by some 28 German fighters and a few scattered anti-aircraft guns. Looking back, anyone with common sense would have realized that the war's outcome was pretty much already decided on the European front, and the firebombing was unnecessary. But, at the time, all of us were too caught up in war fever to think clearly. We went on the mission with great enthusiasm. Unlike many of the previous missions, this one went relatively uneventful. There were very few engagements, and the few outdated flak batteries that defended the city managed to induce only minimal losses on our side. The bombings went on for three days, and at the end, as I looked outside my cockpit, I was astounded to see the level of destruction we had wrought on the city....it appeared to be a scene of the apocalypse."

Jonathan again grew silent and stared blankly, deep in his mind.

"Dad..."

"Oh...Ummm...sorry...just the last part had me thinking...so, uh... where was I?"

"You were talking about the aftermath of the Dresden firebombing, Dad."

"Ah yes...all of us boys were happy with a 'job well done' initially, and back at the base, our brass even held a little party for us with MREs and free cigarettes. However, as the week passed, the real scale of the tragedy we had caused began to unfold. Reading the newspapers, we learned the consequences of our actions: thousands of civilians burned or suffocated to death. We were appalled, but there was little time to gloom over – there was a war to win, and it had to be won if we were to stop further bloodshed. Plus, the word was that the Russians were gaining ground rapidly from the East...now I have nothing but admiration for their sacrifice that helped us win the war...and come to think of it, one of the guys I helped train in flying a P-39 would go on to become an amazing friend of mine...but anyway...the fact was we just couldn't let them have all of Europe under their influence. The war had to be won on our terms. Even at the time, we were aware of the changing world order and that the Russians, then allies, would eventually be our opposition. As the Nazi regime was collapsing, it was a race toward Berlin…and Tokyo. And now comes the most important part…my last mission of the war."

"Dad…I can't wait to hear it!"

"I am sure you can't…now both of you get comfortable in your seat because this part is going to be a long one."

Chapter 6
Operation Cornflakes

The mission I would eventually get to go on would be just as important. They eventually needed another pilot to help with a mission codenamed Operation Cornflakes, and that's where this story begins. Now, we are getting to the best part of the story."

"Please. We are curious, Mr. McKendree. Continue," stated Julia.

"We must've completed about twenty successful missions during this time, but it was on the very last mission that would change my life forever. It was February 5th, 1945, the day after the Yalta Conference, when the UK, the USSR, and the USA decided the post-war world order that was to come. This night started off differently from all the other previous missions. First, I would fly a P-39 Airacobra instead of the usual P-38 Lightening I had normally been flying in these missions. I was told that my plane was down for maintenance and that I would be flying the P-39, and since it had an extra

46

seat, I would be taking on a passenger for training purposes. My passenger was a guy named Daniel Coleman. I didn't think anything of it at the time. I had little reason to be worried. It seemed like a routine affair. I was told I would fly from Bari, Italy, to Linz, Austria, to do our normal mail drop for Operation Cornflakes. Then to Dubendorf airfield in Switzerland to drop off Daniel, my mystery passenger, refuel and then head back to Bari, Italy. No biggie – just standard stuff.

After we completed the maildrop in Linz with no problems, we continued towards Dubendorf airfield. That's when everything went wrong. We started taking on enemy fire, and my worst fears came true. We were hit in the right wing and the engine. At that point, I knew we were going down. There was nothing I could do but try to keep it up long enough to find a spot to land as best I could. I yelled back at Daniel and told him we were going down. I could hear Daniel screaming these words from behind me, 'No matter what happens, make sure these papers get to General Joshua Alexander at Dubendorf. This is of utmost importance. It could decide the outcome of the war. Promise me you will ensure these papers make it if something happens to me. Keep them safe no matter the cost!'

So, it definitely wasn't a routine mission. With so much at stake and the plane crashing, one would go insane with the stress involved. But, strangely enough, I didn't feel any of it. I guess my sense of mission triumphed over all the other feelings I had going through me. I looked for the best place to land the plane but didn't see anything at first. Then I thought the Germans would surely be looking for us, so I saw what looked like a huge lake and decided to ditch the plane there. I knew it would be risky, but I knew I needed to hide the plane the best I could to give us more time to avoid being captured by the Germans. The last thing I remember was hitting the water and then waking up to someone shaking me and asking me if I was alright."

"Oh my gosh, you were shot down and crash-landed in a lake? Where and how did you make it out alive? Why didn't you ever tell us any of this?" Karl asked.

Jonathan did a quick glance at the wall clock.

"Karl, it is getting late. Why don't you come back tomorrow and I can tell you more about what happened? These new meds are really making me tired, and I need more sleep."

"Dad, you can't stop there. Please don't leave us out on the most interesting part. You need to tell us what happened. You can't just leave us hanging like that. We need to hear the rest of the story. What happened to Daniel, and who were the people that found you?"

"I DO intend to tell you the whole story this time, Karl. I need to get this off my chest while I still can. This has been eating at me ever since that day, but your mother and I didn't think it was the right time to tell you."

"Okay, Dad, get some rest, and we will be back first thing in the morning. Lisa will be here to check up on you and give you your meds, and we should be here soon after to finish hearing your story. I need to know how you and Mom met and why it is so important. I guess it's goodbye for now. Take care, Dad."

"Goodbye, Mr. McKendree," Julia said as they made their way to the door.

"See you two in the morning," Jonathan replied.

***

"Knock. Knock. It's me, Lisa. Are you awake yet, Mr. McKendree? I need to get you ready before your son gets here this morning. How did you sleep last night? Are your meds easing the pain for you?"

"Come on in, Lisa. I have been up a while waiting on you, and yes, I slept fine. The meds seem to be working better now. I think they are making me a little more tired, but yes, working much better."

"Would you like me to get you something to eat?"

"Hmmm…well, I could eat some oatmeal and toast. I do think the pain is getting worse now. I will also need my pain meds this morning before Karl and Julia get here. Please do me a favor and don't tell Karl I'm getting worse. He doesn't need to worry any more than he already is. I hope I can hold out long enough to tell Karl everything I need to tell him."

"Jonathan, are you sure you don't want me to tell them? They need to know how bad you are so they can spend more time with you and be more prepared when the time comes. I understand you do not want them to worry about you, but you really don't know how much time you have left."

"I'm sure, Lisa. I don't want them to worry about me. Besides, there's nothing that they can do to stop my cancer. He will have enough to think about after he hears my story. I just hope he will still be around afterward."

"Jonathan, I am sure there is nothing you can tell Karl that will change how he feels about you. I can tell he really loves you by how he acts around you and wants to spend time with you."

"Lisa, I may be an old man, but I am still sane and have only gained more wisdom with my age. There is so much Karl doesn't know that I need to tell him, and I regret not having done it before now.

His mother and I should have told him sooner, and for that, I'm sorry. I wish Lina was here to help me tell him about all of this. I am sure he would have understood so much more if she could have told him instead of me."

"Okay, Jonathan. Have it your way. I will keep this between us for now. I need to get to my next appointment if you don't need anything else today. I will see you again in a few days at our next visit unless you need me sooner. You know how to reach me. Take care. Karl and Julia should be here soon. Don't worry too much about what you need to tell Karl. I am sure he will understand why you have waited so long to tell him once he hears everything you have to say.

"Thanks for everything, and I sure hope you are right. Try to have a good day, and I'll see you next time, Lisa."

Chapter 7
The Crash

"Karl, do you think it's possible that your dad crash-landed in a lake near Germany and was on a secret mission? Or do you think it could be the meds talking? And who is this Old Man Ray and Daniel Coleman? Has he ever mentioned them to you before?" asked Julia.

"I haven't heard of either of them before, unfortunately. I'll be honest with you, Julia; I'm not sure what to believe right now. He and Mom met while living in Germany during World War II, which I'm still processing. I've always been told that they connected after he left the military. Why they kept this a secret is beyond me. It had been forty years since the end of the war. Even though he was on a secret mission, since a lot of time has passed, I would assume that whatever secret he was trying to hide is irrelevant at this point. The statute of limitations for something like this would likely be over by now. So many people from that era are dead; it is all history."

"Well, whatever it is, Karl, it is bothering him. Has he ever been this serious about his stories before? I think it must be something pretty important."

"No. We just always took them for being stories that he made up. None of us ever really took him seriously with his stories. We never really knew when he was telling the truth or not. He was always joking and kidding all the time. Mom would always go along with him, so we just believed him. Now I am starting to question all of the stories he has told. What was real and what wasn't? What is it he could have been trying to protect me from?"

"Remember to keep an open mind about whatever he tells you tomorrow, Karl. Whatever it is, it seems very important that he tells you."

"I will, Julia…" He paused for a moment as he looked out the window towards the lawn. He reminisced about when times were simpler and how quickly time had passed. "He has me wondering if this is him or his meds talking or if some sort of dementia is starting to set in. I hate seeing Dad like this. I am sure he's in a lot of pain and isn't telling us." Julia could see that there was visible remorse in Karl's expression. "I wonder what else he isn't telling us? Maybe I need to talk with Lisa to see what is going on," he added.

The next morning, Karl and Julia were in a hurry, anxious to return to Jonathan's house. They were about to run over each other, trying to get ready.

"Karl, I think I am as curious as you are to see what your dad has to say today. I can't wait to hear the rest of the story and the big secret that they kept from you all these years. I am sure they had a good reason, whatever it was. I wish the boys could be here to hear what your dad has to say. I am sure they would find all of this interesting."

"Yeah, I'm sure they would. But let's hurry so we can get going."

Karl wanted to speak with Lisa when they got to Jonathan's place, but she wasn't there. As he and Julia greeted Jonathan, he informed them that she would arrive a bit later than usual unless there was anything urgent. He wanted to ask Lisa about his dad's illness but decided to wait until she arrived on her own schedule. The couple then chose to hear Jonathan tell the rest of the tale.

"Okay…." Jonathan paused for a good while as the couple anxiously waited. "Hmmm…. I can't remember…. where did we leave off yesterday?"

"You had just crashed the plane in the lake, Dad."

"Oh, yeah, right, the lake. I later found out that it was Lake Chiemsee. Daniel and I had just taken on a few rounds in the right wing, and I thought we would be okay, but then the engine started smoking, and it was just enough to bring us down. I knew we were going down right then, and there was nothing I could do about it. I just started looking for a good place to land the plane, and that's when I saw Lake Chiemsee. It was all that I could see in the woods – this one big old blue lake. Plus, I knew they would be looking for us, so I hoped that the plane would sink and hide the crash from plain sight to give Daniel and me some extra time to maybe get away and have a head start on the Germans. That's the last I remember until I woke up. I was lying in a bed with an older man standing over me as I regained consciousness. He appeared to be in his mid-seventies, and next to him stood a stunning young woman who was roughly my age. I was initially surprised because I was unsure of my location or who they were. They informed me that everything was fine, that I was safe, and that they were there to help when I initially suspected they might be Germans. When I went to sit up, I noticed a splitting headache. I must have had a slight concussion from the plane crash. The older man said his name was Gustav Ryker and that the younger girl was his granddaughter, Lina Martin, your mom. Gustav told me that he was out near the lake when he heard my plane crash and hurried over to help."

Jonathan briefly paused to recollect his memory.

"So mom was there after you crashed!"

"Wow, it sure sounds like a perfect setting for a Hollywood movie, Mr. McKendree," Julia remarked.

"Dad, your story is worth telling as a published autobiography. Why did you and mom choose to hide it for all these years?" Karl inquired.

"Be patient, son... as we move along, you will have the answer to your question," Jonathan replied. "Hmmm...now where was I?"

"What happened, Dad?" Karl asked anxiously.

Chapter 8
The Favor

"I told them my name was Jonathan McKendree, a pilot from the United States with the Army Air Corps, and that the Germans had shot me down."

"You told this to who?" Karl asked. "The guy who was standing at my head when I woke up from the crash," Jonathan said.

"Oh, okay, Dad," Karl said.

"I asked where my friend Daniel was, and Gustav told me that he didn't make it and was still lying by the lake. I quickly asked about the briefcase, remembering what Daniel had said about it and how important it was. As soon as I mentioned it, 'this one?' Gustav asked as he held it up. He had also recovered a few other bags from the plane that must have been floating in the lake. I told him it was very important and that I needed to get it to Dubendorf Airfield as soon as possible. He assured me that he would help me in any way he could to get me on my way to Dubendorf Airfield.

Realizing the briefcase must be important, Gustav removed it from Daniel's dead body and kept it. Hoping to make a deal with me, he asked his granddaughter to leave the room so he and I could talk in private. As soon as Lina was gone from the room, Gustav started in.

'Jonathan, I realize how important this briefcase must be to you, and I'm sure there must be people out there looking for you right now as we speak. Both good and bad. I wish no harm come to you, but I would ask a favor from you for my help and cooperation to get you and this briefcase back to where you need to go.' Said Gustav as he softly placed his left hand on my shoulder to gain more of my sympathy.

'Hold on now, Gustav! I'm unsure what I can or can't promise here, but I need to get going with those papers. Many people's lives depend on me returning them to the Dubendorf Airfield, and I aim to get them there. With or without your help.' I said as I removed Gustav's hand from my shoulder.

60

'Jonathan, I'm an old man now, my health is failing me, and I'm unable to take care of Lina anymore as she needs. I am the only family she has left here now, and the Germans have gotten out of control and need to be stopped. I would like you to take her back to the United States with you so that she will be safe and have a better life. I hope you will consider taking her with you, and in return, I will help you as much as possible to get you and these papers safely to Dubendorf Airfield. I have a friend in the next town who owes me a favor, and he has a truck you can use to get you back to Dubendorf Airfield. I am sure he would be willing to help you if you would do this for me.'

Gustav tried his best to convince me to take his granddaughter with me. While he spoke all of this, he started to feel tired and thirsty. He pointed at the glass and a jug of water lying next to a small table where he was sitting. I understood that Gustav needed some water for his dry throat. I got up from my chair and hurried to pour some water into the glass for the older man.

As I handed the glass of water to Gustav, I said, 'Gustav, even if I agreed to this, I am sure

Lina would never agree, and I wouldn't blame her. You can't expect her to just agree to go off with some complete stranger.'

Gustav took a few sips from the glass of water and spoke, 'Jonathan, let me talk to Lina, and you just think about what I said. We need to start getting things ready and get you on your way before someone else finds out where you are. We don't have much time. Plus, Lina will be able to help guide you on your way back.'

Gustav was really worried for his granddaughter, Lina, and he was looking for someone trustworthy enough to keep her safe. Gustav felt that I was trustworthy enough, given the circumstances, and so he tried his best to convince me.

'Fine, talk with Lina, but I'm sure she probably won't go along with your idea. And who can blame her? She doesn't know me, and it will be dangerous trying to get back with the Germans out looking for us.' I replied.

I excused myself from the house to give Gustav and Lina time to talk privately. Knowing that it would take some time for them to sort out, I told Gustav I was going to the lake to bury Daniel. Plus, it would give me some time to think and take it all in.

While I was alone clearing my head, I kept telling myself that if Lina decided to go, I was doing it for my country. I kept wondering what she would decide as I headed back to Gustav's house after burying Daniel, hoping Lina had talked her grandfather out of his silly idea. I knew I had overstayed my welcome, and I needed to leave right away, with or without Lina. My mind was bombarded with all kinds of thoughts, both good and bad. One part of me wanted Lina to stay with Gustav, while my heart badly wanted her to go with me. I was confused and couldn't decide what to do. "What will I say to Gustav if Lina does agree to go? Will this be a good decision on her part? Should I take her with me? Will I be a good protector? How can I keep her safe? I should honor my word if Gustav trusts me with his only granddaughter." All of these thoughts crossed my mind as I made my way back to the house.

When I reached the house, I found Gustav and Lina sitting in the living room, talking about something. I noticed that they both stopped as soon as I arrived. "Am I here at a bad time?" I asked.

"Certainly not, my friend. We were waiting for you to arrive." Replied Gustav.

"Are you hungry, Jonathan?" he asked.

"Ah, yes. I believe I could eat something," I replied.

"Darling, could you make us some sandwiches? We need to talk about something important while we eat," said Gustav.

Lina rushed toward the kitchen to prepare the food. After a few minutes, she called out to both men to gather around the table. As the three of them took their seats, Gustav spoke, "My dear friend, Jonathan. Have you thought about what we talked about earlier?"

"Yes, I have, but ultimately it's Lina's decision," I replied.

"Lina and I talked about it while you were away. I asked her, and she has agreed to go with you," said Gustav.

Lina and I looked at each other as if she were confirming what Gustav had just said to me. I got my answer.

The house where Gustav and Lina lived was a nice little one on a secluded road outside of town near a small patch of woods. It was white with black shutters on the front and with a little shed out back.

Lina was a very beautiful girl, and I would try my best to keep her safe until we reached the Dubendorf Airfield. I knew the Germans must be out looking for me, and knew it wouldn't be long before I was found.

I knew, good or bad, people were on their way, and didn't want to stick around to see who showed up first.

Chapter 9
The Last Mission

"I was stuck in an area with unknown people around me. I knew I could trust this old man. But I was having a constant fight in my mind.

Something inside was telling me that this would be my last mission. I tried to get a hold of myself and think about what to do next." Jonathan froze, staring out the window in silence.

Karl looks at Jonathan. "Dad, you were telling us about good and bad people on the way to hurt you?"

"Oh, I must have gotten lost again. Kids, I think I need some time to rest now." Jonathan says.

Lisa comes inside the room. "You are looking a bit tired." She starts cleaning the room.

"I think we do need to rest. How about we come back tomorrow?" Julia says while standing up and stretching her legs.

"But, I want to know what happens," Karl insisted.

"I think it would be best to give it a day's rest and relax. If Jonathan feels tired and something happens to him because he is restless, you won't hear the rest of the story, Karl." Lisa said, making a fair point.

Karl nodded and replied in a low voice.

"I guess we all could use a break. Okay, Dad. We'll see you tomorrow." Karl said as he and Julia were leaving the room.

Lisa starts placing everything where it belongs in the room as Jonathan closes his eyes and returns to the lake where he crashed the plane.

He is re-living the moment and replaying everything in his mind. For him, it feels as if he was there. He keeps seeing Lina's face, and he keeps hearing the gunshots. He then has a flashback of himself running into the woods.

The memory became unpleasant for him, and he had to open his eyes to return to reality. "What a life I had," Jonathan mumbled to himself.

"Are you saying something?" Lisa asked.

"No, dear. I am just thinking about the life I had before. Now, I can hardly walk. Back then, I used to be able to do whatever I set my mind to. Here, help me sit up." Jonathan says to Lisa.

"Well, you're older now. You have had a good long life. Cancer takes a toll on everyone. But I am happy you get to talk with Karl and Julia before your time is up." Lisa replies while helping Jonathan sit up.

"Yeah, I do agree. But the life I had haunts me. Sometimes my mind won't stop thinking about all those people who didn't make it through. I think I want to lie back down and sleep. Please give me my pain meds, Lisa." Jonathan says in a disturbing voice.

"Okay, Here they are." She hands him the pills and a glass of water and also helps him lie back down.

"I'll be outside. Ring the bell if you need me." Lisa says and leaves the room.

"I don't need anything. All I need is to tell my son the truth about the last mission." Jonathan mumbles these final words before drifting off into a peaceful sleep.

Chapter 10
The Germans are Coming

"Hey, Dad, we are here," Karl and Julia returned the next morning and woke Jonathan from his deep sleep. He didn't look so well, but was far from giving up.

Both Karl and Julia were hooked as they listened to Jonathan reveal his account of the war and the mission. Taking a brief pause to clear his throat, Jonathan continued:

"I knew I had overstayed my welcome and needed to leave, with or without Lina."

'I had to keep moving, and quick, I kept telling myself as I headed back to Gustav's house after burying Daniel, just hoping for her own sake, Lina had talked her grandfather out of this silly idea of his.'

"Now…thinking about it all, son, in truth, at the back of my mind, I never thought I would be on a secret mission, let alone be taking a beautiful woman with me across many miles of open land with the Germans chasing after us!"

"Dad, this is all so amazing. I can't believe you and mom kept this from me for so long. I still don't know why you and mom never told me this before now. I really wish mom were here to help me understand all of this." Karl said.

"Be patient, son... as we move along, you will have the answer to your question," Jonathan replied. "Hmmm...now where was I? Ah, yes... now, Lina and I both had a lot to think about, but time was a luxury we didn't have. The clock was ticking, and time was running out for both of us. Tick tock, tick tock – the ever-annoying sound of time ticking away in your head when you need it the most," Jonathan narrated as he swung his index finger. He continued, "Time was against me from the moment I crash-landed in the lake, and I needed to get moving to stay ahead of the Germans. Then, my worst fear became a reality."

"What happened, Dad?" Karl asked anxiously.

"I stepped outside for a bit to clear my head and to give them some time to talk. When I started heading back towards the house, I could see lights from way down the road. I thought it odd for people to be out so late. Gustav met me at the door when I got back and yanked me in. I knew right away something was wrong. Gustav said it must be someone coming to look for the plane that was shot down and that we needed to leave fast. He told Lina to go with me out the back door and head towards the old abandoned barn down the road. That would be the direction we would need to head to get back to the airfield. He then handed me the briefcase and my bag and told me to take care of Lina as we had talked. I assured him I would do everything possible to keep her safe.

Lina and I had barely made it out of the house and into the backfield when the cars pulled into Gustav's driveway. We could hear people jumping out of the cars. I'm sure there must've been at least ten soldiers or more. I was holding Lina's hand, and we ran away from there as fast as we could. But, after a fair distance, Lina pulled on my arm and stopped; she didn't want to leave without checking on her grandfather first, so we decided to wait in the field across the road to see what happened. After about five minutes, we heard two gunshots, and that's when I knew we had to go. I told Lina that they must have seen some of my things in the house and knew that I had been there and that he had helped me.

We ran with all we had towards the abandoned barn down the road. Once we got there, Lina was crying uncontrollably. She wanted to go back to the house, but I told her we couldn't and that her grandfather was probably dead. I felt so sorry for her, knowing that she had just lost the only family she had left. I was sad and scared too, but my mind was focused on the mission, and I tried to console myself knowing that, at least, I was fulfilling the old man's wish of keeping Lina safe.

We spent the rest of the night there in the barn, cuddled up because of the cold, with me holding Lina in my arms, trying to stay warm. I don't think I slept that night in the barn because I was shaking from the cold and afraid the Germans would find us. I couldn't believe I had such a beautiful woman in my arms. It was the first time I had really gotten a good look at Lina's beauty while she slept there. She had fallen asleep crying as I held her close. I thought about the first time I saw her. She had the most beautiful eyes I had ever seen, and her smile would melt any man's heart, that I'm sure of. She simply took my breath away, and now here she was, snuggled up in my arms. Just the smell of her seemed to relax me, and the night flew by so quickly. I felt like I was the luckiest man alive at that moment, and nothing outside of the barn seemed to exist. Not the war or even the Germans who were surely still looking for us."

"The next morning was a long day, and Lina pretty much kept to herself; honestly, I couldn't blame her after what happened last night. I tried to console her for the loss of her grandfather. I tried making small talk with her and started sharing details of my life to try to get her to open up and talk, but she kept quiet. I knew it must be tough to lose the only family that you have left. It got me thinking about home and my mother. I wondered what she was doing, how she would feel if something happened to me, and how she would feel if she lost the last of her family. I could vaguely remember back when my father died. I was only about five years old. My mother stayed strong and did not cry at my father's funeral, but I heard her late that night crying. Looking back now, I wished I had gone in there to console her and tell her everything was alright, that she still had me, but I didn't. I'm sure it would be even worse if anything happened to me.

Who would console her now if something did happen to me? I thought. No one, that's who! I had to make sure I made it back home alive to see my mother again. Our only obstacles now were the Germans and time. And they were both closing in fast. We tried staying away from the main roads, following the wood lines to help us blend in as much as possible. Lina said she knew the way we needed to go and also knew an old abandoned house along the way that we could spend the night in, out away from town. After that, she wasn't sure which way to go, and I would have to figure the rest of it out on my own. I just hoped I could figure out which way to go and get us back safe without running into any Germans. In the back of my mind, I was hoping that maybe someone from the base had sent a squad out to look for Daniel and me. If the papers we were carrying were as important as Daniel said, I was sure someone was out there looking. Not knowing who would find us first was the problem."

"Wow. I am not sure what to say...this is already getting so...overwhelming," Karl interjected.

"Believe me, son. This story contains plenty of twists and turns, and we haven't even gotten to the best part yet."

"We're all ears," both Karl and Julia stated.

Chapter 11
On the run

"Your mother had said that if we could reach Kleinmunchen, she knew someone there who had a truck and owed her grandfather a favor. They might be able to reach Dubendorf Airfield with just that. She was willing to help me, which I found hard to believe. I understood that we still had a long way to go before we were safe.

We walked for a long time before arriving in Kleinmunchen. I waited until your mother contacted her grandfather's friend on the outskirts of town. I kept an eye on her to ensure that nothing bad happened to her. Everything appeared to be fine at first, but when she met with Mr. Gruber, things became challenging. He promised to take us as far as he could even though he couldn't give us the truck. He claimed that the Germans were closely monitoring him and that leaving town with the truck would be difficult without them realizing it. He claimed that every day at the same time, the German soldiers took a break.

Our greatest opportunity to get the truck and leave town would be then. When Lina found me again, she informed me that we would need to push the truck a fair distance before we could start it and that we would also need to wait until night before we could take it. So that the Germans wouldn't hear us leaving with the truck, we had to keep quiet.

We felt safe and confident that no one had spotted us until we had traveled a fair distance from town. We mainly discussed the war on the trip— how it had affected everyone and how we were glad it was coming to an end.

We had to return to Dubendorf Airfield. Lina had informed Mr. Gruber. We continued traveling through the night and the following day. I was aware that we would soon need to refuel. Although Mr. Gruber had a few gas cans in the rear, I knew they wouldn't be sufficient to get us all the way to Dubendorf. He said he had a friend who lived in the nearby town who could help us when we stopped for gas at the next station.

We stopped just outside of town once we were close. Mr. Gruber believed it would be more secure. He suggested that Lina and I would go into town to get the gas while he stayed with the truck.

We took a shortcut through the field to attempt to shorten the distance, which also offered me some one-on-one time with Lina to get to know her better. Everything went smoothly, and once he dropped us off, we had enough gas to perhaps get Lina and me to the airstrip in a couple of days. We talked on the walk back while each of us was toting a can. As we drew nearer, I saw that a few automobiles had driven up next to the truck, and they held Mr. Gruber at gunpoint. The following scene left me speechless.

Lina and I were crossing the wide field when I noticed Mr. Gruber pointing toward us. The German officer suddenly shot Mr. Gruber. We came to a complete stop and let go of the gas cans. We turned to head back toward the woods for cover before the Germans could catch us, and I shouted at Lina to run. They must have been tracking us since we left town, I suppose. As we fled, we heard more gunshots coming from behind us.

To avoid being caught by the Germans, we raced as quickly as we could while holding hands. Never in my life have I felt so terrified, I believe. Keeping Lina with me the entire time, I ran as quickly as possible. We made an effort to remain hidden in the bushes. We were aware that we needed to find cover for the evening. We arrived at an old abandoned house just before it got dark. We reasoned that it would serve as the ideal refuge for the night to keep us from freezing.

The house was dilapidated, aged, and worn out. On the house's side, the paint was almost completely gone. Some boards were beginning to break off, and the worn old house was being destroyed by time and weather to the point that there was a sizable hole in the roof. It almost made me think of Old Man Ray's house and the numerous times I had sat with him on the front porch during its better years. Even though it felt like a million miles away, the frigid nights there seemed a lot like the cold nights back home. I just kept thinking I was at least getting closer to home with each step.

Later that evening, I was still working on getting Lina and me situated before deciding to go to bed. I wanted to go outside and look around the house's perimeter to ensure nobody was around. I informed Lina that I would return shortly and asked her not to leave. She told me to hurry back and to be careful. To ensure everything was quiet, I turned and walked out the back door before carefully beginning to ease around the outside. I quickly returned to see how Lina was doing following my brief stroll outdoors. To my astonishment, Lina was gone when I got back. I started to panic right away. I repeatedly called her name until I heard activity in the yard in front of the house. I crept around the back of the house until I came face to face with my worst fear.

Out in front of me, I saw Lina on her knees with her hands up and a German soldier standing over her with a pistol pointed right at her. I could tell she was scared, and I went into protective mode. I lunged for the gun the German was holding and knocked it away, and I yelled for Lina to run as I stood face-to-face with the German. He swung at me, and I dodged his punch, and I punched him in the stomach. He doubled over as I backed off, which was a big mistake. The next thing I saw was a flash of silver in the moonlight. I knew right then he had a knife, and I was in trouble. He swung wildly and missed, but the second swing got me. He cut me on my left side, and I knew I was bleeding. Seeing the fear in my eyes, he took advantage of the situation and jumped at me again, and then he was on top of me. We were soon on the ground, rolling around, fighting for control of the knife. He was on top of me instantly, trying to come down with the knife. I had both hands on the knife fighting with all that I had. While we were about the same size, the soldier tried to use his weight to finish me off with the knife. I could see the determination in his eyes, and I knew that it was now or never. Out of nowhere comes this board hitting the German over the head. With the blood oozing out of my side, I pushed one last time with all I had, turned the knife on the German, and plunged it deep into his chest as he slowly fell onto the ground.

The first thing that went through my head was Lina. She had run back into the house and was curled up in a corner. I could tell she was happy to see me when I walked in. She immediately jumped up, ran straight into my arms, and hugged me so tight I didn't think she would ever let go. Then she kissed me. All she kept saying was, I'm sorry. I'm sorry. I was shocked at first, but then I just took it all in and didn't want to ever let her go. I could have stayed right there forever with her in my arms.

She looked down and saw that I was bleeding and immediately started ripping at the bottom hem of her dress. She folded it as a makeshift bandage and tied a long piece around my waist to hold it in place. I noticed she was shaking badly as she tried to bandage me up. I grabbed her hands and told her I was ok, then wrapped my arms around her and held her tight. She hugged me back. Right then, I knew I never wanted to be without her. I whispered in her ear, "I guess now I owe you a new dress." She just laughed and started to relax a little.

I told her we better hurry up and get moving. I'm sure that was a scout, and when he doesn't return, we will have a whole German army after us. She grabbed my hand, helped me up, and we headed out of that old house. I can still see it in my head. It just looked like an old rustic house with all of the windows busted out of it, the roof had many shingles missing, and the front door was gone. You could tell it was a nice house at one time. My mother and I would gladly have lived in that house when it was new. Our house was so rough looking, but she did what she could to keep a roof over our heads.

"I hated watching your grandmother Beth struggle in the manner that she did when I was a child. I thought it was my fault that she was having so much trouble. I believe she may have secretly entertained thoughts of marrying Old Man Ray if she had been alone. She might not have, just to protect me from men who might harm or abuse me out of respect for my dad. Your grandmother was a wonderful, courageous woman. Looking back now, I realize all of the many sacrifices that she made for me."

Chapter 12
The Rescue

"'I never told you, but thanks for saving me last night,' your mom said while looking at the ground. 'You don't know how much that means to me. I was so scared. I thought I was going to die right then and there,' she said.

'Well, you saved me too. He probably would have killed me if you hadn't hit him over the head with that board. Come to think of it. He probably would have killed both of us. Plus, you bandaged me up and stopped my bleeding.'

'Jonathan, can I ask you a question?' Lina said with a curious look on her face.

'Sure, Lina. You can ask me anything. You know that. I will answer it if I can.'

'What did you and my grandfather talk about the night he got shot before we left?'

'He made me promise that I would ensure that you were safe and that nothing would happen to you. He also asked me if I would take you to the United States.'

'And what did you tell him? Surely you knew you couldn't promise me passage to America without us being married.'

'At that moment, I was willing to promise your grandfather just about anything to let me get out of there and back to the base. I figured when it was time, you would have to decide whether you would stay here or go with me. I was going to let you decide. I just knew I had to get you away from there and try to keep you safe.'

'What did you think I would do? Did you think I would go?'

'Lina, I didn't know what you would do. I just knew I wanted to keep you safe like I promised your grandfather. But I wasn't sure what you would decide once we got there.'"

"A small platoon ambushed your mother and me just as we were about to arrive at Dubendorf airfield. I initially believed it to be the Germans, but it turned out to be a small platoon of Americans. We joined them to avoid being caught by the Germans. The soldiers were cordial toward us. We accompanied them the rest of the way to Dubendorf."

"Lieutenant Samuel Gregory was in charge of this team. They were sent out to locate us and retrieve the top-secret documents from the briefcase before the Germans could. I realized we were secure at that point, and this nightmare was almost over. Since the day we went missing, they had been searching for us, according to Lieutenant Samuel Gregory. They had lost track of us on the radio. When Daniel and I failed to arrive at the base after being dispatched, they quickly realized something was wrong. He claimed they had come across a small group of Germans who they believed were searching for us. He warned that they needed to move quickly if they wanted to find us before the Germans did. On our way back to Dubendorf, I told him of our close call with the one German and that I knew they were close to finding us. He said that he knew. I asked how did you know? He said that was how they found us, by following the bodies. They had found Gustav at the house, Mr. Gruber on the road, and then the dead German at the old abandoned house. They knew they had to hurry because the Germans were closing in."

"Once we arrived at the base, I was taken to General Joshua Alexander. Lina was taken to a room so she could rest for a while. The general greeted me and was relieved to see that the briefcase was still with me. We began talking about the briefcase, and I told him everything that had happened before the small platoon found us. After we had resolved everything, I started questioning him about what would happen to Lina and whether she could return to the United States with me. There was no way I could leave her behind, as she was now my responsibility. He informed me that unless she was married to an American, there was no way he could permit her to go to the United States. He inquired as to our plans for marriage. We hadn't discussed it, and I informed him that I wasn't certain she felt the same about me as I did about her. He assured me she would be sent back to the United States if we decided to get married. If we came to that decision, he even had a Chaplain on base who could marry us right away. I told him I needed time to speak with Lina and explain the situation to her. Take your time, he advised; you will be here for a while until I am debriefed on the mission," Jonathan paused.

"I'm so amazed at everything you have been through. I can't believe you kept this a secret for so long," Julia says while pouring herself some water.

"Yeah, Dad, how come you never told me about this in all these years?" Karl asked.

"Well, I never found the right time to talk with you about all of this, and I was unsure about how you would feel," Jonathan responded.

"I'm glad we are getting to hear this from you now," Karl said.

Chapter 13
She said, "Yes."

"I stopped by Lina's room, and she was sleeping. So, I decided it was best to talk with her in the morning. I went back to my room. I wanted to take a nice hot bath and get something to eat before sleeping. It felt awkward to me. I never thought I would get married under such crazy circumstances. But this was an out-of-control situation for both of us. She had nobody to look after her anymore, and somehow, I blamed myself."

"Were you afraid that she would say no to you?" Karl asked.

"I somehow knew the answer before I even asked your mother. I was in love with her, and there was no way that I was leaving her behind. However, I knew I could convince her if something else were on her mind." Jonathan responded.

"So, what happened the next morning?" Asked Julia.

"We had been running for a long time, and it was days since we had eaten a proper meal. Finally, we were taken to the base canteen and had a peaceful breakfast.

After both Lina and I finished eating, I asked her to come for a walk with me. So, we walked towards the outer perimeter of the base to have some privacy. I told her about my meeting with the General and how everything would be okay now. She listened to me as if she knew what I was going to ask next.

"I began discussing the General's information with your mother and laid out her options. I assured her that the United States Army would ensure the Germans were gone and safely transport her back home. I also informed her that the Army would only permit her to go to the United States if she was married to an American GI. I confessed to her my feelings and that I had fallen in love with her the moment I saw her, adding that it was her choice whether or not to get married. And I could accept it if she didn't feel the same and decided to return home. To my surprise, she pulled me aside and started telling me how she felt the same about me, but there was something she needed to tell me before I made my decision."

"I took her by the hand, looked deep into her eyes, and said, Lina, if it is about your past, it doesn't matter to me. The General said there was a Chaplain here on the base, and we could get married immediately, and he would ensure your arrival to the United States. I love you and want to spend the rest of my life with you. Will you marry me?"

"So, you didn't even listen to what mom was going to tell you?" Karl asked.

"No, Karl. It didn't bother me. I just wanted us to be together, no matter what."

"So what happened next?" Julia asked.

"Well, we didn't know it at the time, but the people on the base were so excited that they had already planned a huge celebration even before Lina had given me her yes. It gave them a reason to be happy during such a trying time." Jonathan replied.

"Lina responded yes, and the excitement spread like wildfire throughout the base. The

General's staff all circled to congratulate us," Jonathan said.

"Your stories are getting better, Dad. I wish Mom were here with us," said Karl.

"Yes, Karl, I agree with you on this one. This journey without your mom being here has been indeed difficult. I wish she were here while I told you, kids, the story of our lives," Jonathan said.

"So, you got married, and she was sent to the United States?" Julia asked.

"We got married, but this story has a twist," Jonathan said.

Chapter 14
Good-bye for now

"Once we were married at Dubendorf airfield, the General assured me that he would guarantee that Lina would make it to France to get aboard the S.S. Argentina that leaves for South Hampton and then off to New York. That was the ship assigned to take all the brides safely back to the United States. I gave my dog tags to your mother and kissed her farewell, telling her I would see her soon. I still had to stay back and finish with my account of what happened and ensure that the papers were finally delivered where they were supposed to be and sent safely. Duty comes first; this is why the General didn't allow me to go with your mother even after all we had been through. I had to keep my oath to protect my nation and obey the General's orders. Also, the ship was for brides only. I wasn't happy about this. At least Lina could go on to the United States, where I knew she would be safe while she waited for me. I would have to finish my debriefing before I returned to New York to see your mother again.

I could tell she didn't want to go without me, but I assured her that I would see her soon and that we would be together. Telling her goodbye that day was one of the most difficult things I'd ever had to do—especially the next day after just getting married," Jonathan returned to the gallery of his memories of when he was waving goodbye to Lina.

'I will be with you soon,' I said.

'I will wait for you. But, please do come back home,' Lina said.

'I will, my love,' I said while kissing Lina on the forehead.

I said my goodbyes and realized how much I loved your mother. So, I finished up, seeing her off at the airfield in Dubendorf aboard a plane headed for France, and then we met back up in New York after I finished my account with General Alexander. I have never spent a night apart from her ever since. I made sure of that. I wanted to be home with her, and as much as she was scared of losing me, I felt the same."

"Okay, Dad. I have to ask. Did you ever look inside the briefcase to see what was so important?" asked Karl.

With a serious voice, Jonathan said, "Karl, I can't tell you what those papers were. You know that!" He chuckled and said, "That's top secret. Of course, I peeked inside. Why wouldn't I? If I didn't, what kind of person would I be? I needed to know what was in that briefcase that was so crucial that my life and your mother's were on the line. I was shocked by what my eyes saw when I looked inside that briefcase. I nearly fell over then and there."

When he thought back to the crash, Jonathan almost felt like he was there, holding the top-secret documents in awe. The result of the war might have changed if people had known what he was holding. He was aware that he needed to move quickly.

"Well, Dad, what was in there? What were the documents about that made them so important?"

"They were top-secret documents about the atomic bomb drop. As soon as I saw it, I was in disbelief. Knowing I couldn't bring these papers back to base, I sat there trembling. I realized that the entire nation depended on me at that very moment."

Jonathan described how the best times, dates, and locations to deliver the atomic bomb were revealed by the top-secret papers in the briefcase. "Additionally, the bomb would be carried by a B-29 bomber named the Enola Gay. That was the key factor. We might not have won the war if we didn't have this knowledge. Without these papers, neither the length of the war nor its outcome is known. Daniel sacrificed his life so that those documents could reach the Dubendorf airfield. And I was prepared to sacrifice the same for our nation."

"All right, Dad, I suppose I understand the need for confidentiality surrounding the documents in the briefcase, but that was so long ago. You won't get into any trouble now, I'm confident. What is the major secret, then? That can't be everything. What's the rest of the story? Is any of this even true?"

"Every bit of what I have told you is the absolute truth, so let me continue," Jonathan answered.

"I must say that your mother played her part in saving the country too. She knew the importance of the papers, and she told me if something were to happen to either of us, one of us would carry on and complete the mission." Jonathan said.

"Even when your mother and I were not married, we still shared a good understanding with each other. Even though she was not an American and was living in Germany, she didn't back off and walked step by step with me to make sure we reached the base." Jonathan further explained.

"Well, Dad. I always heard different stories from you and Mom. Sometimes, you two conversed with each other, and I couldn't understand. But now I think both of you knew what you were talking about. So, I feel it's a puzzle that I completed today. Huh? There was so much I didn't know and understand then," Karl said.

"Okay, Dad. I now understand the secrecy of the papers in the briefcase. So, what's the big secret that you have to tell me? That can't be all of it." Karl asked his father as he was about to discover something he was not expecting.

"Well, Karl. You are right. This is not everything that I have to tell you. This last thing I have to tell you, I want you to know that it changes nothing between you, me, and your mother." Jonathan replied to Karl. Whereas Julia sat quietly, wondering what it could be.

"Karl. What I am about to tell you is that...." Jonathan paused for a while before saying it.

Chapter 15
What's in the Box

Jonathan smiled. He knew where his son was going with this. Suddenly, his face dropped, and he nodded. He continued to speak, "Karl, I can see that you probably don't believe me, but what I am telling you is the God's honest truth. Let's just settle this once and for all. Go into my bedroom and look up at the top of my closet. There you will find a small wooden box in the upper right-hand corner. Get it down and bring it in here to me. This will answer a lot of questions for you."

Karl went into Jonathan's bedroom and returned after just a few minutes with an old cigar box. "Here, Dad, is this the box you were talking about?" He handed the box to his dad; the lump in his throat grew after he said that. Karl was wide-eyed with curiosity at what could be in the small box.

"That's the one. The two of you come, sit here beside me on the bed, so I can show you what's in here. These are some of the things I have left from when I was in the military."

Karl and Julia glanced at each other with confused looks on their faces, wondering what could be in the box that could clear all of this up; after all, it was just an old cigar box that had been sitting in his bedroom forever. What could be so important about it? Karl and Julia were young and naïve; they had no idea what such little things, as a cigar box, could conceal.

Julia asked Karl if he had ever seen this box before.

Karl, a little unsure, shook his head. Although he had seen a cigar box in his dad's bedroom before, he had never paid attention to it. What was there to pay attention to anyway; the type of wood it was made up of or its size? "I guess?" He recalled.

Jonathan looked up at them with a smile on his face like a kid opening presents on Christmas Day. Even though he already knew what was hidden inside, he couldn't wait to show them his old treasures waiting to be rediscovered.

As Jonathan opened the box, it was as if a time machine had transported him back to the moment he first put the objects in there. All those emotions came flooding back to him as if it was 1945 again; everything was on repeat before his rattled eyes, the battleground that stayed witness to the bloodshed, the men who fought valiantly, and the guns that blasted through the serenity. It made Jonathan emotional, and a tear rolled down his cheek. Were his tears not enough evidence for Karl and Julia to take the dying man seriously?

Karl and Julia, baffled, had to say his name a few times to snap him back to continue.

"Sorry," Jonathan apologized and wiped the tear. "Just brings back a lot of memories."

The first thing he pulled out of the box was a white-handled dagger with German markings on it.

"Is this the dagger you got cut by and killed the German with?" Karl asked.

"Yes, it is Karl. Your mother didn't want me to keep it. I looked and looked for the gun, but I couldn't find it in the dark. I didn't have any other protection, so I kept the knife with me until we got back to Dubendorf airfield, and I've had it since that night." A cold chill ran through Jonathan as he pulled up his shirt to show him the four-inch scar he had on his side and lay the knife there. "This is the first time this knife has touched me since that night."

Karl reached out in disbelief as he touched the knife and the scar to make sure that he wasn't seeing things. Julia was now at a loss for words as she just looked on in awe staring at the knife. She didn't know what to say or how to process everything she had witnessed right before her eyes.

"Now that I have your attention, let me show you what else I have in my box." Jonathan reached in to grab another item.

Karl and Julia were excited. Anticipation grew with every second that wavered, waiting for what was next.

What Jonathan pulled out next fit in the palm of his hand, and they couldn't see what he held until he reached out to Karl and told him to hold out his hand. Julia became attentive as Karl stretched his hand out. Then, Jonathan dropped what was in his hand, which further confirmed what Jonathan told them about the knife. It was a dog tag with a German name on it. Karl showed it to Julia, who touched it in disbelief. It read: *Heinrich Kasner*.

"I only took the one. I left the other on his body so his people would know who he was. Your mom never knew I took it. She probably wouldn't have approved if she had known," said Jonathan. Jonathan reached in again and pulled out a handful of pictures this time. He fumbled through them until he found the one he was looking for. "H-here it is," he said.

He handed Karl a picture. At first, he hesitated, but when he looked at it, he couldn't believe what he was looking at. While Karl was looking at the picture, Jonathan was still flipping through more of the old photos; he was still searching for that one big hoorah.

104

"Is that Mom? And is that the S.S. Argentina? Is that the ship she came over here on?" asked Karl with tears in his eyes.

What Karl held in his hand intrigued Julia. She leaned in to get a closer look at the photo, and her eyes widened. She couldn't believe it. Was that really Karl's Mom?

At that moment, all that prevailed was silence and wonder in their minds.

"Oh, and here is another I want you to see," Jonathan stated as he handed him another photo. Karl looked at it and saw his dad standing in front of a P-39 airplane. "That plane is a real piece of history, Karl, and I don't mean it because it's old."

"What do you mean by that?"

"Well, son, that is the P-39 Daniel, and I was shot down in. The one still sitting at the bottom of Lake Chiemsee, continue listening; there is so much more you need to know."

"This is all too much to take in. How much more can there be?" replied Karl.

Chapter 16
The Big Secret

Jonathan showed them the letter he had received from the Office of Strategic Services (OSS), thanking him for his bravery and commitment to the service of his country. The letter was signed by the head of the OSS and the President of the United States of America, Harry S. Truman. Karl and Julia were amazed and couldn't believe that the letter Jonathan had shown them was real. They looked at each other, and Karl didn't know what to say, but he still had some unanswered questions.

"Did they ever ask you where the plane was and what happened to Daniel?" Karl asked.

"Yes, they asked me about the plane and Daniel. I told them I didn't know where I crash-landed due to my concussion and told them that Daniel was dead. I'm unsure if they ever went looking for the downed plane, but I know they never found Daniel's body, which has haunted me my entire life. He should be brought home and buried with honors."

"Now, Karl, this is the hardest thing for me to say. I hope you can forgive me for not telling you before now. When I first met your mother, she was already pregnant. I'm not your biological father. The day we got married at Dubendorf Airfield, your mother told me that she had to tell me something significant before we decided to get married. This was when she told me she was pregnant and that I probably wouldn't want to be with her. I didn't care if she was pregnant or not. I loved your mother more than anything in the world. And you know I have always loved you like you were my son. I always wanted to tell you the truth, but your mother wouldn't let me. What you don't know is that after we got back, we got married and had a big reception, just like we told you. But about a year after you were born, your mother and I tried to have a child of our own together. But no matter how hard we tried, we could not have one. Your mother could see my disappointment, and that's when she told me that you have a son, which should be good enough for both of us. She said if it wasn't for her grandfather and me bringing her back to the United States, the two of us probably wouldn't have made it there with the Germans. So, I had more than earned the right to be your father. I asked if she was sure about this. And all she could do was cry and say she was sorry for not giving me a child. I was good with her decision and loved you as if you were my own. I have loved you since the day you were born, which was good enough for me.

"So, if you're not my father, then who is? What happened to him?" Karl asked in disappointment.

"His name was Karl Greiner. As I said earlier, I made sure; your mother named you after your father. He was killed by the Germans not long before I had crash-landed in Lake Chiemsee. Your mother didn't have a chance to tell your father about you before the Germans killed him," Jonathan said.

Karl and Julia were speechless. They couldn't believe what they had just heard. Karl got up, shaking his head, and walked out the door, saying, "It can't be true. Why wouldn't you tell me the truth?" Why didn't Mom tell me?" Karl got a little loud.

Julia got up and followed Karl to console him. She knew this was a lot of information to digest all at once. She felt as shocked as Karl.

"Karl, are you okay? Do you really believe all of what your father has said?" Julia asked.

"Julia, I don't know what to believe now because of what he has told me. All of this is starting to run together with all of the other stories I heard growing up. I do believe some of it is true, but I am not sure all of it is. I guess we need to go back in there and see what else he has to tell me. I'm just not sure how to process all of this. It will take me some time," Karl said.

"Well, the big question is if all of this is true, does that change the way you feel about him? If he's not your real father?" Julia asked.

"I don't really know how or what to think about all of this. I need to go back in and talk to him to find out more. Then maybe I can try to understand what happened and why mom never told me all of this if it's true. Let's go back inside and try to figure this all out," Karl responded.

Julia and Karl go back into the living room. Jonathan could see the disbelief on their faces.

"Karl, I have one small request of you. Find Daniel's family and tell them what happened to him and where to find his body. He is buried near a big boulder on the lower southwest side of Lake Chiemsee. It won't be hard to find. I think it's time Daniel came home to be with his family. He has been gone far too long. They need to know the true story of what happened to him. It was only because I was taking Daniel to Dubendorf Airfield that I got shot down and met your mother. It is crazy how one small ripple in time can change your life forever. Whether for good or bad, the effects can be ever-lasting," Jonathan said. Karl slowly believed Jonathan and reflected on the stories he had observed since childhood.

"Karl, promise me you will make sure Daniel is found and that he makes it back home, so his story can be told. He deserves to be with his family after all of these years," Jonathan said again.

"I promise we will make sure they find him, and they get to hear the story of what happened to you and Daniel. One other thing," Karl said.

"What's that, Karl?" Jonathan asked.

"I love you, Dad. Now get some rest," Karl said with tears in his eyes.

Jonathan slowly closed his eyes to sleep with a smile on his face. He said, "Now, my mission is finally complete. I love you too, son."

A LIFETIME OF LOVE THAT'S A BOND THAT CAN'T BE BROKEN.

THERE IS NOTHING LIKE A PARENT'S LOVE FOR THEIR CHILD, BUT THE BOND A FATHER AND SON CAN MAKE AT A YOUNG AGE CAN LAST A LIFETIME.

"FLY'EM HIGH, DO OR DIE."

Epilogue

In the following months, the military recovered Daniel's remains with the help of Jonathan's directions. They found Daniel right where Jonathan had said he had buried him, near the boulder by Lake Chiemsee. Daniel's story was finally told, and he received a hero's welcome in his hometown, where he was awarded the Medal of Honor.